■ EASY START ■

# A day by the sea

Series editor: Keith Gaines

Illustrated by Tony Kenyon

Nelson

"Let's all go to the sea,"
said Sam.
"Would you like to go
for a day by the sea?"

"Yes, we would,"
they said.

"I am going to walk there,"
said Sam.

He started to walk.

"I am going to run there,"
said Ben.

He started to run.

"I am going to go on my bike," said Meg.

She got on her bike.

"I am going to go by car,"
said Deb.

She got in her car.

"I am going to go by train," said Jip.

He got on the train.

"I am going to fly there,"
said Pat the pig.

"You can't fly there,"
said Sam.

"Pigs can't fly."

"Here I am,"
said Jip.

"Here I am,"
said Deb.

"Here I am,"
said Meg.

"Here I am,"
said Ben.

"Here I am,"
said Sam.

"Where is Pat the pig?"
said Jip.

"Pat the pig is going to fly,"
said Sam.

15

"Here I am,"
said Pat the pig.
"Pigs can fly."